SAD.

For my mom. Without her, I'm sad.
—M. I. B.

For Cathy Rutland, who makes me happy
—D. R. O.

SIMON & SCHUSTER BOOKS FOR YOUNG READERS
An imprint of Simon & Schuster Children's Publishing Division
1230 Avenue of the Americas, New York, New York 10020
SIMON & SCHUSTER BOOKS FOR YOUNG READERS is a trademark of Simon & Schuster, Inc.
For information about special discounts for bulk purchases, please contact Simon & Schuster Special Sales
at 1-866-506-1949 or business@simonandschuster.com.
The Simon & Schuster Speakers Bureau can bring authors to your live event. For more information or to book an event,
contact the Simon & Schuster Speakers Bureau at 1-866-248-3049 or visit our website at www.simonspeakers.com.
Book design by Laurent Linn
The text for this book was set in Joppa, Cronos Pro, and Cafeteria.
The illustrations for this book were rendered digitally.
Manufactured in China
0318 SCP
First Edition
2 4 6 8 10 9 7 5 3 1
CIP data for this book is available from the Library of Congress.
ISBN 978-1-4814-7627-0
ISBN 978-1-4814-7628-7 (eBook)

I'M SAD

By Michael Ian Black

Illustrated by Debbie Ridpath Ohi

SIMON & SCHUSTER BOOKS FOR YOUNG READERS

New York London Toronto Sydney New Delhi

I'm sad.

Will I **always** feel like this?

I don't think so.

I was sad once.

I didn't know **potatoes**
could be **sad**.

Everybody feels
sad sometimes.

Even astronauts?

Even astronauts.

If I was an astronaut, I would never be sad.

Why do sad things happen?

That's just the way it is.

But **why** is that just the way it is?

Because if it were any other way, then **that** would be the way it is and it's not that way. It's this way.

That doesn't make any sense at all.

Sigh.

Sigh.

Sigh.

Flamingo, I think you need some good old-fashioned cheering up.

ICE CREAM!!!

Flamingos don't eat ice cream.

Potatoes don't eat ice cream.

DIR

Dirt and soil are the same thing, Potato.

Thought maybe I'd fool you.

I'm still sad.

Maybe it's **okay** just to be sad.

Why would that be okay?

Sometimes when I'm sad, it feels kind of **good** to let myself be **sad**.

Will you still like me if
I'm sad again tomorrow?

I don't like you just
when you're happy.
I like you all the time.
When you're sad or angry
or bored or anything else.

That was really funny.

Do you still
feel sad?

I still feel a little bit sad,
but I also feel
a little bit better.

And I think I'm okay with that.

SAD?